Give Thanks to the LORD

Written by **Karma Wilson**

Illustrated by **Amy June Bates**

ZONDERVAN.COM/
AUTHOR**TRACKER**

zonderkidz
The children's group
of Zondervan

www.zonderkidz.com

Requests for information should be addressed to:
Grand Rapids, Michigan 49530

Library of Congress Cataloging-in-Publication Data
Wilson, Karma.
   Give thanks to the Lord : celebrating Psalm 92 / written by
Karma Wilson ; illustrated by Amy Bates.
      p. cm.
   ISBN-13: 978-0-310-71118-6 (jacketed hardcover)
   ISBN-10: 0-310-71118-5 (jacketed hardcover) 1. Bible. O.T.
Psalms XCII–Meditations–Juvenile literature. 2. Thanksgiving Day–
Juvenile poetry. I. Bates, Amy June, ill. II. Title.
   BS145092nd .W55 2007
   242'.62–dc22
                                                   2006001929

Published in association with Writer's House.

Editor: Bruce Nuffer
Art Direction and Design: Laura Maitner-Mason

Illustrations used in this book were created using watercolors.
The body text for this book is set in Century Old Style.

Printed in China

07 08 09 10 11 • 10 9 8 7 6 5 4 3 2 1

To my children, Michael, David, and Chrissy. Every day I give thanks to the LORD for creating them
— K.W.

For my mom and dad
— A.B.

Celebrating Scripture
Psalm 92
It is good to praise the LORD and make music to your name, O Most High.

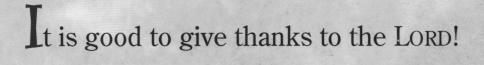
It is good to give thanks to the LORD!

Friends and family here at last.
Hugs and kisses all around.
Everybody says, "Hello!"
Laughter makes a merry sound.

The day is lovely, cool, and bright.
Our house is filled with noisy cheer.
A perfect day for giving thanks
as we all gather here.

It is good to give thanks to the LORD!

Outside the leaves are piled high,
red and yellow, gold and brown.
We climb our way up to the top
then laugh and roll back down.

We shiver in the autumn breeze.
It's blowing in a gusty storm.
We're called into the cozy house
for cider sweet and warm.

The house fills up with tempting smells—
turkey, stuffing, yummy pies!
And just when we can't wait much more,
"It's ready!" Mama cries.

We all sit down, we all join hands.
Our heads are bowed as we say grace.
We give our highest praise to God
and feel him in this place.

It's good to give thanks to the LORD!

Food and fun and family,
all the wonderful things I see,
God has given these to me.
I'm just as grateful as I can be.

The table makes a lovely sight.
The food is good, it tastes just right.
I savor every single bite.
I feel so full of love tonight.

I gobble up my pumpkin pie.
Grandpa laughs and says, "Oh my!"
I can't eat more, but still I try,
`til finally I sit back and sigh.

And when the wondrous meal is done
we chat and laugh and sit a spell.
Everyone has jokes to share;
everyone has tales to tell.

I'm so tired I have to yawn
as we all say our sad goodbyes.
I climb in bed, whisper prayers,
get a good-night kiss, and shut my eyes.

And it's good, so good to give thanks to the LORD.